Willie the Worm

MICHAEL L. STAHL

ISBN: 978-1-64314-793-2 (Paperback)
        978-1-64314-794-9 (Hardback)

Library of Congress Control Number: 2023901784

AuthorsPress
California, USA
www.authorspress.com

AN ADVENTURE OF
WILLIE THE WORM
AND
HIS FRIENDS
WESLEY THE WASP
WENDELL THE WEASEL
WILLIAM THE WARTHOG
AND
WALTER THE WOODPECKER

By Michael L. Stahl

DEDICATION

To my amazing twin
children,
David and Deborah

Every so often something happens that is totally unexpected. So it was with the birth of David and Deborah, as neither my wife Carmen, all of her doctors, as well as myself, were aware of the fact that my wife was carrying twins. Consequently, the sound of only one heartbeat was detected.

Willie The Worm was walking by the Winsome Woods one warm and windy day when he spotted his friend, Walter The Woodpecker pecking on the wood-bark of the great walnut tree. Willie The Worm wistfully wished that he could fly like his friend Walter The Woodpecker pecking on the wood bark of the great walnut tree.

When William The Warthog walked by and asked Willie The Worm, what he had planned to do this day, as it was Wednesday, and he finished all of the work around the house his mother had wished him to finish.

"Hi," replied Willie The Worm to William The Warthog, "I was just about to discuss that with Walter The Woodpecker, who is perched over there on the great walnut tree." Then Willie The Worm called to Walter The Woodpecker and asked, "Hi Walter The Woodpecker, would you like to join William The Warthog and me for a walk through the Winsome Woods?" "Yes I would" answered Walter The Woodpecker, as he flew down from the great walnut tree. And just as Walter The Woodpecker was flying down to talk to Willie The Worm and William The Warthog, Wesley The Wasp came buzzing by. When Wesley The Wasp saw his friends as he flew by he asked, "What are you three planning on doing this windy Wednesday afternoon?"

William The Warthog answered, "We are all going for a walk through the Winsome Woods, and would you like to join us?" "Wonderful," said Wesley The Wasp, "I would love to join you for a walk through the Winsome Woods."

And so Willie The Worm, Walter The Woodpecker, William The Warthog, and Wesley The Wasp entered the Winsome Woods on this beautiful Wednesday afternoon, for a peaceful walk; but not knowing that they were in for an exciting adventure.

About fifteen minutes into their walk, as they were telling each other funny stories they met Wendell The Weasel with a very worried look on his face. "Why do you have that worried look on your face?" asked Wesley The Wasp. "Well," replied Wendell The Weasel, "I was just watching how those wild dark clouds are wandering in as the approaching winter wind is wickedly starting to blow hard. And where there are dark clouds there is usually loud thunder and scary lightening, as well as lots of rain."

"Wow," said Wesley The Weasel. "The wind really is starting to blow a little wild and gusty, and it does look like it is going to rain very hard; and if we do not get home right away, we are going to get wet and chilled to the bone."

"No, no." said William The Warthog. "I'm not afraid of some wind, and we don't really know if it is going to rain, so let's continue our walk". And so Willie The Worm, Walter The Woodpecker, William The Warthog, Wesley The Wasp, and Wendell The Weasel, even though a little nervous, continued their walk down the winding path deeper and deeper into the Winsome Woods.

Willie The Worm was not paying attention or looking where he was walking, and before he knew it he had stepped onto a spider's web.

This alerted Spindly The Spider, and she started a smooth slide down her web towards Willie The Worm as he was a tasty looking worm. Willie The Worm started to scream, "Save me, please somebody save me from Spindly The Spider. She would like to make a meal out of me." It was then that Walter The Woodpecker flew across the winding path and bit the spider web in half, picked up Willie The Worm in his beak, and deposited him between Walter The Warthog and Wendell The Weasel's feet.

Willie The Worm who was now a little shaken up, told everyone how frightened he was when he saw Spindly The Spider coming towards him; and how thankful he was for Walter The Woodpecker coming to his rescue. "I will be very careful where I walk from now on" said Willie The Worm.

As they continued their walk they talked about the beautiful wild flowers that grew beside the winding path they were walking on. The flowers came in so many different colors and shapes. Some were red and some were yellow. In fact they came in all of the colors of the rainbow as well as beautiful flowers that had splashes of different colors on them. And how very big the trees grew in this part of the Winsome Woods! In fact, some of the trees looked so tall and big that you had to take several steps sideways just so you could see what was on the other side of them.

Wesley The Wasp just thought the butterflies had the most colorful wings, and looked as graceful as a sunbeam as they danced from flower to flower, tasting the sweet nectar from every flower they landed on.

Wesley The Wasp looked at his sparkling clear wings and said to Wendell The Weasel, "I wish that my wings were as colorful and as beautiful as the ones that the butterflies have. Butterfly wings are so beautiful and graceful." Wendell The Weasel looked at Wesley The Wasp and said, "Be careful what you wish for; they might look pretty, but you are much safer from things that like to eat wasps, as your sparkling clear wings make you harder to see."

"That is a very good point," said Wesley The Wasp to Wendell The Weasel. "I am now quite happy with my sparkling clear wings."

They were all walking along, enjoying the walk and each other's company when Walter The Woodpecker, while looking up to talk to William The Warthog, tripped on a smooth but bumpy rock. "Hay, watch where you are walking" came a voice from the rock to everyone's amazement. "That's no rock" said Wesley The Wesel. "That's Timothy The Turtle." "Timothy The Turtle, what are you doing so far away from the Peaceful Pond?" asked Walter The Warthog. "I decided to take a walk, but with the wind starting to blow hard and the sky getting dark from those gray clouds rolling in, I became a little lost, and cannot find my way back to the Peaceful Pond. Do any of you know the way back to the Peaceful Pond?" asked Timothy The Turtle.

"With my sensitive nose, if I wish to, I can smell the water in the Peaceful Pond," Wendell The Weasel announced as he pointed his nose up in the air, and started to sniff the wind. "If we make a right turn from where we are now standing, we should run right into the Peaceful Pond." Wendell The Weasel announced.

And so Willie The Worm, Walter The Woodpecker, William The Warthog, Wesley The wasp, Wendell The Weasel, and Timothy The Turtle all made a right turn, and started walking towards the Peaceful Pond.

After several minutes of walking, Walter The Woodpecker took off and flew above the tall bushes and chirped, "There it is. I can see the Peaceful Pond just ahead in the direction we are walking. Timothy The Turtle, you are almost home". Everyone was so happy they all started to cheer as finally Timothy The Turtle, was no longer lost, and they all knew how happy he would be to once again, be swimming with his family, in his beautiful, Peaceful Pond.

Now that Timothy The Turtle was once again safe at home, Willie The Worm, Wesley The Wasp, Wendell The Weasel, Walter The Woodpecker, and William The Warthog decided to explore the area around the Peaceful Pond. As the five friends were walking around the Peaceful Pond, Walter The Warthog exclaimed, "Look what a beautiful color blue the peaceful pond is, why everything is so calm and restful here." And just as Walter The Warthog finished talking, up out of the Peaceful Pond walked Alcazar The Alligator.

"Well hello, I am Alcazar The Alligator," said Alcazar The Alligator. "I am a friendly alligator and what a nice group of friends you all are. All of my friends have moved away and I am very lonely. I would like to be your friend. Why don't you all come into the Peaceful Pond for a lovely swim on this warm day? It will cool you off, and will be so much fun." Said Alcazar The Alligator, in his deep, smooth-talking voice.

Walter The Warthog became very suspicious, especially when he saw how big Alcazar The Alligator's teeth were. "No thank you," replied Walter The Warthog, it is getting late and we have a long walk home." When Walter The Warthog said this, Alcazar The Alligator opened his mouth very wide and ran towards Wendell The Weasel, as he was closer to the Peaceful Pond. But Wendell The Weasel was very quick to step back, as he did not want to get caught by Alcazar The Alligator. With seeing how dangerous Alcazar The Alligator was, the five friends very quickly ran back through the Winsome Woods to the winding path, so that they could go back to their walk through the Winsome Woods, on the winding path.

They were walking for about twenty minutes when right in front of them, Snicker The Snake, dropped down from one of the lower branches of a great tree, with his tongue slithering in and out of his mouth. "And where do you all think you are going?" asked Snicker The Snake, while giving Wendell The Weasel a flash of his golden eyes, thinking that Wendell The Weasel just might make a delicious dinner. Walter The Warthog sizing up the situation, bravely put himself between Snicker The Snake and his friends and said, "If I were you, Snicker The Snake, I would just slither away, or you will feel just how sharp my tusks are."

"You do not frighten me Walter The Warthog", said Snicker The Snake. "My teeth are just as sharp as your tusks, and I will not slither away." As fast as a blink of your eye, Walter The Warthog grabbed the nose of Snicker The Snake, and yelled for Wendell The Weasel to get Snicker The Snake's tail so they could tie him up in a knot. And that is just what they did.

They then carefully picked him up and put him in the bushes on the side of the path, knowing that it would take him a very long time to untie himself. And just as though nothing had happened, the friends continued their walk on the winding path in the Winsome Woods. Several minutes later as they continued their walk, they felt the first drops of a very chilly rain. "Oh my goodness" said Walter The Woodpecker, "we are so far from home, and I fear that it is going to be a really bad downpour, and we are probably all going to get soaked to the bone." Just then Wesley The Wasp noticed a very old great spruce tree that had fallen over. Wesley The Wasp said to Wendell The Weasel, "Why don't you run over there and see if that great old spruce tree is hollow? If it is, we can all go inside the tree and rest while we wait for the rain to stop." And sure enough, the old spruce tree had hollowed out as it had been down for so long. Now the rain was really starting to come down hard.

Walter The Woodpecker picked up Willy The Worm in his beak and flew with Wesley The Wasp as Wendell The Weasel and William The Warthog ran over to the great old spruce tree that had fallen over. Once inside the tree everyone felt so snug and cozy. It was really fun, and they all started to laugh, and once again started to tell funny stories as the rain came down harder and harder. It only took several minutes, and the rain started to slow down, and finally it stopped altogether. So the friends left the comfort of the great old spruce tree, and started walking down the path once more.

They were only walking about five minutes when they heard this growling, with the growling getting louder, and finally the loudest growling that really sounded more and more like snarling. It was then that they realized that it was the nasty growling of Wilfred The Wild White Wolf. "Oh my goodness" wailed Wendell The Weasel. "Wilfred The Wild White Wolf will make us his dinner. We must hurry and get to the safety of our homes."

So Willie The Worm crawled onto the back of Wendell The Weasel. Walter The Woodpecker and Wesley The Wasp could fly, so they felt that it would be much easier for them to escape from Wilfred The Wild White Wolf by flying instead of walking.

William The Warthog and Wendell The Weasel with Willie The Worm on his back, began to run as fast as they could on the winding path in the direction leading out of the Winsome Woods. It was then that they heard the crash of Wilfred The Wild White Wolf smashing through the Winsome Woods. They all knew that this was very bad for their safety, and they began to run faster and faster towards home on the winding path through the Winsome Woods.

Just as they were approaching a large curve on the path in the Winsome Woods, there was a very big rumble of thunder, and a very loud crackling sound as a huge bolt of lightning struck one of the largest evergreen trees in the Winsome Woods. The great evergreen tree came crashing down right across the winding path that would lead them on their way out of the Winsome Woods, and to the safety of their homes.

"Oh, what shall we do?" wailed Wendell The Weasel, "What shall we do?" "Wilfred The Wild White Wolf is coming our way. I can hear him getting closer and closer." William The Warthog looked at Wendell The Weasel and said, "Do not worry, I will burrow a small tunnel under that great evergreen tree just so that only we can fit through. Wilfred The Wild White Wolf is so big he will never be able to fit through the opening in the tunnel that I will make". And so William The Warthog began to dig as fast as he could. "Oh." Wendell The Weasel said, "Dig faster, dig faster, Wilfred The Wild White Wolf is almost here, please dig as fast as you can under the great evergreen tree."

And there he was. A monster of a wolf. He was so much bigger than Wendell The Weasel remembered. His eyes a bright, glowing red, like wildfire. Large white teeth that looked as sharp as a knife, and a wicked, menacing snarl, coming from deep down in his throat. Walter The Woodpecker and Wesley The Wasp immediately flew over the great evergreen tree as Wilfred The Wild White Wolf began a menacing slow walk towards Wendell The Weasel.

William The Warthog noticing this, really began digging as fast as he could under the great evergreen tree. There was sand and dirt just flying everywhere through the air as he dug faster and faster. Finally he was through to the other side of the great evergreen tree just as Wilfred The Wild White Wolf leaped in the air to pounce on Wendell The Weasel for his dinner. Then William The Warthog grabbed Wendell The Weasel's tail in his mouth, and dragged him through the tunnel to the other side of the great evergreen tree.

There was no way that Wilfred The Wild White Wolf was able to squeeze through the small tunnel that William The Warthog had dug under the great evergreen tree. And you were able to hear Wilfred The Wild White Wolf growling and howling, and growling and growling as loud as he could, as he was not able to squeeze through the tunnel that William The Warthog dug under the great evergreen tree. He was not going to have a tasty dinner this evening, and he was so angry that he began to scream as loud as he could.

Everyone met at the home of Wendell The Weasel that evening to celebrate their great adventure thanks to William The Warthog. This is an adventure that Willie The Worm, Walter The Woodpecker, William The Warthog, Wesley The Wasp, and Wendell The Weasel will tell over and over to their friends for a very long time. It was a great adventure how five friends escaped from Wilfred The Wild White Wolf.

CPSIA information can be obtained
at www.ICGtesting.com
Printed in the USA
BVHW012110260223
659239BV00011B/410